Once Upon a Playground

by Jack Frakes

SAMUEL FRENCH

Please refer to page 30 for further copyright information.

CAST OF CHARACTERS

WANDA BUN

TOOTIE SHOE

DIDI FEE

FORDA MOORE

PHOEBE DIVE

DIXIE WICKS

FLIRT STEVENS

GEORGIE

THE GIRL

THE BOY

PLACE

A playground—an almost bare stage.

SETTING

One ladder, two platforms: one large, one small, about a foot high; two benches and some rings hanging from above.

TIME

The present—late in the afternoon.

DESCRIPTION OF CHARACTERS

All the characters are relatively the same age. The unusual names come from numbering the girls, again trying to find a point between realism and theatricalism.

WANDA BUN *is a tall girl and the leader.*

TOOTIE SHOE *is thin and tiny. She's been sick. She follows Wanda.*

DIDI FEE *has to wear corrective shoes.*

FORDA MOORE *is a little fat, but she has a sense of humor.*

PHOEBE DIVE *has to wear glasses.*

DIXIE WICKS *has to wear braces on her teeth. She's also a leader, but not as strong as Wanda.*

FLIRT STEVENS *is a little bit dumb. She could even stutter.*

GEORGIE *is a dreamer and story teller.*

THE GIRL, *Jill, is the "Girl with the Funny Nose."*

THE BOY, *Johnny, is the "Boy with the Funny Nose."*

Basically, the girls' costumes should suggest—either realistically or theatrically—tomboys. They generally wear jeans, sweatshirts, baseball caps and tennis shoes. However, there may be deviations from this. They could either be real or a costumer could carefully plan gradations of color which could unite them. The boys could wear white shirts, dark pants, perhaps sweaters and bowties. Or Georgie could suggest more of the Mother Goose rhyme of Georgie-Porgie and wear brightly colored stripes or plaids.

Braces for Dixie may be drawn on with black tooth enamel.

Nose putty can be used for the noses on the Girl and the Boy.

The only other special items are a black eye and "corrective" shoes for Didi.

Once Upon a Playground

The LIGHTS come up on seven girls in sweatshirts, jeans and baseball caps who are spontaneously arranged on ladder, platform and ground. They are posing in boyish, somewhat "frozen" postures, and staring front. Throughout the play, there is a mixture of realism and theatricalism, both vocally and physically. A GIRL WITH A FUNNY NOSE enters Down Right kicking an old beaten up tin can. She stops.

ALL. (*Together.*)
>Once upon a playground,
>Where the whole gang goes
>To meet and hang around,
>Came a girl with a Funny Nose.

DIDI, FORDA, PHOEBE *and* FLIRT. Girl with a Funny Nose.

DIXIE. Funny Nose.

WANDA. (*Cynically.*) Nose . . . Funny!

ALL. (*The* GROUP *laughs and each runs in a different direction.*) Ha, ha, ha, ha, ha! (*They stop in their new positions and say together:*) ONCE UPON A PLAYGROUND!

PHOEBE. Hey, everybody, let's play baseball!

ALL. (*Ad-libbing—separately.*) Okay. First up! Second! I had first. Who's third? (*Etc.*)

DIXIE. No, let's choose sides.

WANDA. I'll choose first. I'll choose Tootie Shoe.

DIXIE. Didi Fee. (*Pronounced "DeeDee."*)

WANDA. Forda Moore.

DIXIE. Phoebe Dive. (*Pronounced "Feebee."*)

WANDA. (*Last, and least.*) All right, come on, Flirt.

GIRL. Can I play?

WANDA. No.

GIRL. Why not?

ALL. (*Forming two lines.*) Because you're different. (*They all waggle their fingers from the end of their noses.*) You've got a funny nose. (*Pointing at her.*) You're different. (*They move Upstage Left and Right into two huddled groups with heads together and down as they speak. Echoing softly.*) Different. (*Softer yet.*) Different. (*Softest.*) Different.

(*When each of the girls speaks her inner thoughts and fears—an expressionistic technique—it is to herself and the audience. The others "do not hear" and their reaction, vocally and physically, exists only in the mind of the girl speaking her inner thoughts.*)

GIRL. I don't want to be different. Oh, why do I have to have a funny nose? Why? Sometimes I get desperate thoughts. (*She walks as if walking along a line, balancing herself.*) Once I even got the scissors out and I almost cut it off so it'd look just like everybody else's. But I was afraid I might mess up the whole thing, and it'd look even worse than if I left it alone just the way I was born with it. (*She jumps up on small platform.*) So I left it alone. And that was probably best since they were pinking shears. (*She jumps down off small platform.*) But, sometimes I get so sick of being different I could scream. Then, out of somewhere I dream of a boy —a boy who has a funny nose just like mine—a boy whose name is Johnny.

ALL. Johnny be nimble, Johnny be quick, Johnny jump over the candlestick.

GIRL. Johnny, the *boy* with a funny nose.

DIXIE. (*Popping her head up.*) Funny nose. (*She ducks down again.*)

WANDA. (*Popping her head up; cynically.*) Nose . . . Funny!

ALL. Ha, ha, ha.

GIRL. But why Johnny? The name keeps going through my mind, but he's only a dream. Oh, why do some of us have to be different and alone? Why?

ALL. (*Building down—echoing.*) Why? Why?

GIRL. (*Crossing toward bench at Left.*) Why alone and different? I just don't understand. (GIRL *sits on the bench.*)

DIXIE. Okay, Wanda, you chose first, so we get to go to bat first.

WANDA. I tell you one thing . . . I can play baseball just as good as any of those old *boys*.

TOOTIE. Yeah, and probably better.

DIDI. I'll tell you another thing—I'll *never* like boys again.

WANDA. Me, neither. That's why I treat them as bad as I can—just to be sure they'll never like me.

PHOEBE. I think boys are *so* silly.

DIDI. Yeah, that's for sure. Say, Phoebe, how's your brother been lately?

PHOEBE. Nasty as ever. Why?

DIDI. Oh, no reason. Just wondered.

TOOTIE. You know what I try to do with my brother. I get every bit of information I can against him, so when he does anything mean to me, I can get even with him. That way, it ends up making me the person who's right.

PHOEBE. Yeah, that's what I do, too.

FORDA. Come on, you guys, let's play.

WANDA. Okay, Dixie, get your team organized. Come on, team, and I'll decide who's gonna play what.

(*They go into two huddles again:* WANDA'S TEAM *goes Up Right and* DIXIE'S TEAM *goes Up Left. Almost immediately,* PHOEBE DIVE *steps out of the group and moves forward and squints at the audience.*)

PHOEBE. Oh, there you are. I can't see a thing without my glasses. Not a single thing. But I just hate to wear them. I look awful with them on—just awful.

ALL. Awful. Just awful.

PHOEBE. (*Jumping up on large platform.*) Here, I'll show you what I look like. (*She puts chinning rings in front of her eyes.*) See? I do look awful, don't I? (*She lets them snap back.*) Anyway, I'm always embarrassed to tears when I have to see the blackboard. I can see it if I squint real hard, but I don't like to squint. Then, everyone knows you can't see. One day I squinted so much the boy across the aisle started calling me "Squintzy."

(TOOTIE *and* FLIRT *look up, squint, and say:*)

TOOTIE *and* FLIRT. Hiiiii, Squintzy.

PHOEBE. (*Jumping down from platform.*) If I started wearing my glasses all the time and looking awful like I do, the other girls would think I was different. And they wouldn't want me to hang around any more. I don't wanna be different. So I just pretend I can see just fine, when I can't see anything at all. (*She bends over and surveys around.*) The whole world looks like a fuzzy blur to me. But I'm not different.

(*She moves back toward Dixie's group and crashes into the ladder en route.* TOOTIE SHOE *moves out from Wanda's group immediately.*)

TOOTIE. I been sick a lot. Boy, if there's one thing I hate, it's being sick. Seems like I've always been sick and skinny and run down. (*She coughs.*) I've tried everything to get well:
"Early to bed, early to rise,
Makes you healthy, wealthy and wise."
But no healthy . . . no wealthy . . . no wisey.
You know the old saying: "An apple a day keeps the doctor away"?

ALL. An onion a day keeps everybody away.

TOOTIE. Well, for almost a month I ate an apple a day to keep the doctor away. I've never been so sick in my whole life. I used to go from one cold to another. (*She blows her nose.*) And I had to stay home from school all the time. That means you have to play alone. And sometimes you think it's kinda fun. But if you're really honest, you're lonesome . . . and different. Nobody wants to be different, so when I'm well and with the girls in the neighborhood, I go along with just about anything they wanna do. I'm always afraid I'm gonna get sick for a long time and they'll forget me forever. I just hate to be sick. (*She coughs or sneezes.*)

WANDA. Okay, our team's ready.

FLIRT. But I don't wanna play out in the field all *alone*. Anybody got any comic books?

DIDI. Sure, here.

PHOEBE. How'd you get them out?

DIDI. My mom doesn't care just as long as I don't read too many.

WANDA. You know, I just figured out—I got around five hundred comic books at home.

TOOTIE. My mom makes such a fuss I have to hide mine.

FLIRT. My "Superman" is missing, and I think my mom burned it.

PHOEBE. Hey, whatcha got to trade?

DIDI. I'm all through with my "Little Orphan Annies."

PHOEBE. Oh, boy, I'll trade you for a "Bugs Bunny."

DIXIE. I'm tired of comic books. You guys can have all of mine.

ALL. Oh, boy! Hey, neat. Swell. Etc.

DIXIE. Only on one condition . . . I can read them whenever I want.

ALL. (*Ad-libbing, separately.*) Sure, oh, boy. Hey, that's neat. Swell—"Little Orphan Annie." "Little Lulu." "Superman"!

GIRL. (*Rising from bench.*) Can I read one of those comic books?

DIDI. No.

GIRL. Why not?

WANDA. 'Cause you don't belong.

TOOTIE. You're different.
ALL. You don't belong!

(THE GIRL *dejectedly sits again.*)

FORDA. (*Moving Down Center and standing full back.*) Hey, you guys, I'm hungry. I feel like having a double fudge sundae with whip cream and walnuts. Let's go down to the drugstore.
WANDA. We just came from there. I had a butter-scotch sundae with everything.
FLIRT. Yeah, and I had three candy bars.
PHOEBE. I had four.
FLIRT. I could eat another one.
TOOTIE. My mother won't let me have anything except popsicles.
FORDA. Then have a popsicle.
TOOTIE. I already had five!
WANDA. Aw, I don't wanna go back to the drugstore tonight. I'd rather just stay here and talk.
PHOEBE, TOOTIE *and* FLIRT. (*Ad-libbing, separately.*) Sure. Okay. It doesn't matter.
GIRL. (*To* FORDA.) I'll go with you.
FORDA. (*Turning toward the* GIRL.) I don't want to go, anyway. And even if I did I wouldn't let you go with me.
GIRL. What's your name?
FORDA. (*Facing full front.*)
      Puddin' tame—
      Ask me again and I'll tell you the same.
GIRL. I won't bother you at the drugstore. Cross my heart and hope to die. Just let me go with you.
FORDA. I said no!
FORDA *and* TOOTIE. No, no, a thousand times no!
ALL. We'd rather die than say yes.

(*All the* GIRLS *quickly line up tightly against each other side by side facing front, and the ones on the end put their hands on their hips. This is to give the stylized idea that it is one fat girl. All of them puff up their cheeks with air and look bulgy-eyed—staring front. Meantime, the* GIRL *crosses back to the bench and sits.)*

FORDA. (*Facing front, talking directly to audience.*) You know, I eat too much! I guess it's obvious. I don't really want to, but sometimes I just can't stop myself. I just wanna eat and eat and eat. Sometimes I eat almost anything and everything—like one afternoon I ate a whole jar of onions and a chocolate sundae in twenty minutes. Boy, did I feel sick!

ALL.

> Fatty, fatty, two by four—
> (*Moving heads from side to side.*)
> Swinging on the kitchen door—
> (*They stop.*)
> When the door began to shake,
> Fatty had a bellyache.

FORDA. Yeah, you know—lots of gas. One day my Mom was having a bridge party and I made a loud belch right there in front of everybody. But I always say: "It's better to belch and bear the shame, than squelch the belch and bear the pain." I've tried to lose weight. . . . No candy, no ice cream, no potatoes. . . . No fun! I might as well be dead. Sometimes I worry about it. I don't wanna be fat and different. I wish I was thin. No, I wish everybody else was fat. Then, e could all be miserable together!

ALL. (*Returning to normal places with* DIDI *standing on the large platform.*) Ooooooh, miserable!

GIRL. (*Rising.*) I don't think she's so fat.

WANDA. Hey, you—beat it!—Or else.

GIRL. (*Innocently.*) Or else what?

WANDA. Did you hear what Didi did? She beat up Johnny Line?

DIXIE. (*Admiringly.*) Hey, good goin', Didi!

DIDI. Yeah, look, I got a real neat black eye. But you oughta see *him*. Powie in the kisser!

Dixie. Boy, that'll sure show them.

All Girls. (*Ad-libbing agreement—separately.*) You said it. Boy-and-how. I'll tell you.

Girl. What's *your* name?

Didi.

> Buster Brown—
> Ask me again
> And I'll knock *you* down.

(Didi *jumps off the platform and stumbles.*)

Wanda. Boy, Didi, you may be the toughest girl in the neighborhood, but you're also the clumsiest.

Didi. I can't help it. (*She moves to talk to the audience.*) If I had one wish in the world it would be to throw these old corrective shoes in the garbage can. (*She steps up on the Downstage platform.*) All the kids make fun of them because they're big and funny. They call them clodhoppers and gunboats.

All. (*All march clumpingly Upstage and stand pigeon-toed with heads down. One is on ladder with her foot extended onto another's shoulder.*) Clodhoppers. Gunboats. Pontoons.

Didi. But I can't help it if I have to wear them. I got my feet from my mother, that's all. She has awful feet . . . fallen arches and great big bunions. But my Mom says if I'm real good to my feet and wear these lousy shoes, then my feet'll be husky and healthy when I grow up. But who wants husky feet? I sure don't. (*She jumps down and does a little "twinkle-toe" step.*) I'd rather wear pretty shoes and get callouses and bunions and just suffer. I don't mind suffering. (*She limps.*) I do it all the time. You know, I think they make these kind of shoes ugly just on purpose so you'll think they're doing you a lot of good. I mean, nobody would ever make shoes this ugly by accident. (*She sits on Upstage platform.*) I can hardly wait till summer comes so I can run around bare-footed, (*She puts feet in air and pedals bicycle fashion.*) and I won't have to wear these clodhoppers. Nobody else wears them— (*She stops and rises.*) I don't see why I have to!

(DIDI *crosses back to her position.* TOOTIE *and* FORDA *move and sit on bench at Right.* PHOEBE *and* DIXIE *move to sit on big platform. The other* FOUR *gather in a group.*)

DIXIE. I wanna play cards. Come on, Phoebe, let's play poker.

(PHOEBE *and* DIXIE *begin to play cards and the* GIRL *crosses over to them.*)

PHOEBE. I'll ante two matchsticks.
GIRL. Hi. (*They don't answer, but instead continue to play.*) Can I play? I wanna play. I won't be in the way. I just wanna play.
DIXIE. (*Dealing cards.*) No. Go away. You can't play.
PHOEBE. We just wanna play by ourselves. We're having fun this way, hey?
DIXIE. Yeah, hey, so go away.
PHOEBE. (*Rising.*) You cheated! You pulled a card off the bottom. I saw you, you cheated!
DIXIE. (*Rising.*) I didn't, either!
PHOEBE. You did, too! I saw you. (*Jumping up and down.*) Dixie is a cheater! Dixie is a cheater!
DIXIE. You take that back, Phoebe Dive, or I'll skin you alive!
PHOEBE. (*To the* GIRL.) She did so cheat, didn't she?
DIXIE. You can't take her word for anything. She's just a lousy pest! Tell her I didn't cheat and you can play.
GIRL. (*Pauses.*) I don't think I wanna play. It doesn't sound like much fun and you're not very nice. (*She quietly returns to her bench.*)
DIXIE. (*She looks after her and then turns to the audience.*) I don't know why I act like that. I guess I try to hurt other people before they hurt me. Or maybe it's 'cause of my parents. You know, sometimes parents get real lousy ideas what's good for you. Like these braces for my teeth, for instance. It seems that my main prob-

lem was I had too many teeth in my mouth. They made all my teeth stick out in front—you know, buck teeth. So they pulled out four teeth and put these lousy braces on, along with some stupid headgear that I have to wear every night so my jaw won't move. It feels like I got a mouth full of metal. You know, fancy grillwork. And every time I smile I feel like I've got a tin grin. (*She smiles insipidly.*) So I try to keep my upper lip down over the braces so no one will notice.

ALL. So no one will notice.

DIXIE. And my parents said, "All the other kids have them." Ha, all the other kids! I only know one girl that has them—Lulubelle Dinklehoffer—and everybody thinks she's a real pill—me, included. And then my parents said, "They'll only be on for three years." Three years! How long do they think I'm gonna live?! (DIXIE *returns to her position.*)

WANDA. You *know*, I been wanting a gearshift bike. *You* know, like the fellows, but my mom won't let me have one yet.

PHOEBE. I want a horse, but Mom says we can't keep it in the house. So—

DIXIE. That's the way moms are.

DIDI. My dad's my buddy. We get along just swell.

FLIRT. I think my Dad's just about the best daddy in the whole world.

FORDA. So do I.

TOOTIE. I hate my dad! He's always so mean to mom and me. Won't let us go any place or do anything.

GIRL. My dad's never even at home.

FLIRT. Nobody asked you.

WANDA. And besides, you've got a funny nose.

FLIRT. Yeah, you've got a funny nose. (*She laughs and points at* GIRL.)

GIRL. That's sure a childish thing to say. Any two-year-old can see I have a funny nose. Boy, are you dumb!

FLIRT. *Dumb?* (*She turns and climbs first step of ladder.*)

ALL. (*Moving into groups; looking idiotic.*) Dumb diddely dumb-dumb . . . dumb-dumb!

FLIRT. (*Climbing up ladder.*) Oh, I wish I weren't so dumb. All my friends are smart. And my mother thinks *I* should be making real good grades in all my subjects, too. But I'm just not smart and that's a fact.

ALL. If dumbness were an occupation, she'd be a great sensation.

FLIRT. But who wants a dumb friend? I'm just scared all to pieces that some day all those girls will find out I'm dumb and different and they won't let me be one of the gang any more. (*She leans sadly on top of ladder.*)

WANDA. I'm tired of baseball.

TOOTIE. Me, too.

FORDA. I'm tired, too, Tootie.

DIXIE. We haven't even played yet.

WANDA. I'm tired of it, anyway.

TOOTIE, FORDA, PHOEBE, DIDI *and* FLIRT. (*Ad-libbing agreement; separately.*) Me, too. So am I. That's right. I don't wanna play. Let's forget it.

DIXIE. Boy! Talk about rats deserting a sinking ship.

WANDA. I know what let's do.

TOOTIE. What let's do?

WANDA. (*She jumps up on Center platform.*) Let's play King on the Mountain.

ALL. (*Ad-libbing; separately.*) Okay, let's go. Let's play King on the Mountain.

(FLIRT *climbs down from ladder.*)

GIRL. Can I play?

DIDI. Naw. We don't wanna play with a girl with a funny nose!

FORD, PHOEBE *and* FLIRT. Girl with a funny nose.

DIXIE. Funny nose.

WANDA. (*Cynically.*) Nose . . . Funny!

ALL. (*They all laugh; separately.*) Ha, ha, ha, ha, ha!

WANDA. Wait! I don't see why it would hurt to let her play King on the Mountain. Remember what happens to the King?

ALL. (*Nodding knowingly.*) Ummmm—huhhh.

TOOTIE. Yeahhhhh, I remember.

WANDA. Sooooo . . . ?

ALL. (*Ad-libbing; separately.*) Sure. Why not? Yeah, let her play.

GIRL. But what do I do?

WANDA. (*Jumping down and crossing to her.*) You're the king.

GIRL. The king?

FORDA. The king.

DIXIE. King Funny Nose! (ALL *laugh.*)

WANDA. And you stand on that platform over there and don't let anybody get up there. Understand?

GIRL. (*Crossing to the platform.*) I'll try. I'll do my very best.

PHOEBE. We couldn't ask for any more, could we girls? (*They all smile cruelly. The GIRL gets on top of the "Mountain." They surround it and slowly circle her.*)

DIXIE. There she is—King Funny Nose.

ALL. Down with King Funny Nose! (*They start slowly and increase their speed as they circle her and continue to jeer and taunt her noisily. Ad-libbing—separately.*) Ha, ha. Down with King Funny Nose. The Girl who's different. (*Then, suddenly someone from behind pushes her, she turns and faces them, but then, someone from behind again pushes her. They shove her this way and that and jeer and taunt her until WANDA jumps up on the platform and shoves her off onto the ground. She stands on top of the "mountain" as all the girls look down on the GIRL.*)

WANDA. You had enough? (*No answer.*) Girls with funny noses just can't play. And you're a girl with a funny nose.

PHOEBE, FORDA *and* FLIRT. Girl with a funny nose.

DIXIE. Funny nose.

WANDA. (*Cynically.*) Nose . . . Funny!

ALL. (*Jeering laughter.*) Ha, ha, ha, ha, ha!!!

WANDA. Why don't you run peddle your papers?

GIRL. Because I don't have any papers to peddle.

WANDA. Nobody likes a smart aleck. Me in particular.

ALL. Nobody likes a smart aleck. (*Echoing; softly, softer, softest.*) Smart aleck . . . smart aleck . . . smart aleck . . . (*They go into new positions.*)

WANDA. That's what my mother says to me. She doesn't like me very much. She always liked my sister better. My sister's the pretty one and the "young lady" of the family. But I'll get even with her. I'll show her. (WANDA *crosses over by the ladder; underneath, peering out, if it's tall enough.*)

ALL. I'll show her. Show her . . . show her . . . show her.

WANDA. You see, the whole reason my mother hates me is because I'm so much taller. When I was born my mother took one look at me and thought I was part giraffe. My mother keeps harping at me to stand up straight.

ALL. (*Almost sounding like a parrot.*) Stand up straight, Wanda. Stand up straight.

WANDA. But when everybody you talk to is two feet shorter, what're you gonna do? You know those dances in P.E. class. I hate them—I really hate them. The teachers think they're doing us a big favor—getting us "socially adjusted."

ALL. (*Deep, sincere tones.*) Socially adjusted.

WANDA. So the boys stand on one side of the cafeteria and the girls stand on the other. And if you're lucky, nobody'll ask you to dance. I'm usually lucky. But I'll never forget one Friday . . . some "good-hearted" pipsqueak came over. I knew if I didn't say yes I'd get graded down for being "uncooperative." And he was the "funny" type. He looked up and said, "How's the weather up there?" Well, I fixed him. I just leaned my chin on the top of his head, relaxed, and he collapsed on the floor. (ALL *laugh.*) See, you're laughing, too—just like my mother. But I'll show her. I'll get even. They're not gonna hurt me. No one!

ALL. No one!

DIXIE. Hey, listen, I heard a neat joke today. (*They*

all huddle in a circle and the GIRL *gets up and slowly crosses back to the bench again.*) You see there was this boy and girl . . .

(*They make a buzzing sound like bees. Then* PHOEBE *lifts her head.*)

PHOEBE. You mean, they aren't brought by the stork?
ALL. No!
DIXIE. Of course not, silly.

(*They all go back into the huddle and buzz again. Then they* ALL *laugh except* PHOEBE.)

PHOEBE. I don't get it.
DIXIE. What don't you understand?
PHOEBE. What that word means. I looked it up in the dictionary and it wasn't even listed. (DIXIE *whispers it in her ear.* PHOEBE *laughs.*) Oh, now I get it. That's pretty funny.
WANDA. I've got one. (*They all buzz again.*)
TOOTIE, PHOEBE *and* FLIRT. (*Together.*) What do you know about that?
TOOTIE. Well!—I'll tell you one thing—*I'm* never gonna get married.
ALL. (*Ad-libbing, separately.*) Me, neither. Yeah, that's for sure. Boy, I'll say.
FLIRT. (*Bewilderingly.*) Oh! I don't believe a word of it. (*My* parents would never do *that.*)
PHOEBE. (Mine, neither.)
WANDA. Listen, I've got another one. . . . (*They* ALL *start to put their heads together again.*)
FORDA. Hey, here comes Georgie.
ALL. Georgie! Here comes Georgie!
PHOEBE. Which Georgie?
GEORGE. (*Entering at Right.*) Nice Georgie.
WANDA. Crazy Georgie.
GEORGIE. That's a fine thing to say, Wanda Bun.
ALL. (ALL *except* WANDA *run over and kneel at his*

feet, with their backs to the audience.) Fee fie foe fum, give us a piece of chewing gum.

GEORGIE. Here, have all you want.

ALL. (*Busy among themselves.*)

> Oh boy, how swell, how dandy.
> Now give us a piece of candy.

GEORGIE. You probably won't believe me . . . *but* . . . once I ate eight pieces of bubble gum all at once.

ALL. We don't believe you. (WANDA *crosses underneath ladder again.*)

WANDA. And what's so good about that?

GEORGIE. If you think it's so easy, try it sometime. (*He crosses to the ladder, climbs to the top and sits facing front.*)

TOOTIE. Don't fall, Georgie!

GEORGIE. Who, me? Don't be silly. This reminds me of the time I sat on the ledge of the "Umpire" State Building . . . just before I parachuted down.

WANDA. You've never even been in New York.

GEORGIE. No, no, I was sitting on top of the "Umpire" State Building . . . in San Francisco.

ALL. Ohhhhhhh . . . !

GEORGIE. Yeah, and it's 400 stories high. Four hundred and five to be exact. And I was on the very top. Well, all the reporters were standing around and they said to me . . . "George" . . . They called me by my first name. . . . "Georgie, before you jump, tell us how you made your touchdown in the big game. Tell us how you knocked that homer in the last of the ninth." Yes, sir, those were the days.

TOOTIE, PHOEBE *and* FLIRT. So, what happened?

GEORGIE. So, I jumped. Haven't you ever heard of Georgie, the Jumping Giant?

WANDA. No, and you've never even been in San Francisco, either.

GEORGIE. I have so.

WANDA. All right, then, where is it?

GEORGIE. On the southern coast of Kansas, so there!

WANDA. Ha! That's all you know about it.

TOOTIE. What else have you done? Tell us some more stories.

ALL. (*Except* WANDA.) Yeah, tell us some more.

WANDA. He hasn't done anything.

ALL. He has, too.

GEORGIE. Did I ever tell you about my secret mission?

TOOTIE. No, Georgie, tell us.

GEORGIE. It was the year when I was an international spy. I was playing my guitar in the garden of the imperial palace when this real cute, beautiful girl walked out on the balcony. She was a spy, too, only I didn't know it. Her lips were like a red, red rose. And her hair was like spun gold. And her eyes were like ebony stars.

WANDA. Ebony is black.

PHOEBE. She had two black eyes?

GEORGIE. Why do you always have to be so technical?

ALL. Wan-da's a kill-joy. Wan-da's a kill-joy.

WANDA. He read all that in a book.

GEORGIE. No, I didn't. I saw it in a movie. It was the second feature at the Paramount. (*All the* GIRLS *groan, disappointed, and turn away, their dream destroyed.*)

ALL. Oh, Georgie.

GEORGIE. All right, all right. You make up something better.

WANDA. (*To* GIRLS, *getting out from under ladder and crossing to above* GIRLS.) You see. I told you. He makes up everything. Nothing like that ever happened to Georgie and never will.

GEORGIE. That's all you know, Wanda Bun. In spring anything can happen. Anything.

WANDA. I have an idea. Come here. (*They* ALL *crawl on their knees the short distance to* WANDA. WANDA *whispers and they giggle.*) Georgie, we dare you.

GEORGIE. (*Getting down from ladder.*) Dare me to do what? (*All the other* GIRLS *rise and cross to* GEORGIE.)

TOOTIE *and* PHOEBE. We double dare you.

DIDI *and* FORDA. Double dare.

FLIRT *and* DIXIE. Double dare!

GEORGIE. To do what?

WANDA. Listen! (*They circle* GEORGIE, *whisper in his ear and point toward the* GIRL.)

GEORGIE. I accept the dare, the double dare, the triple dare. So there! (GEORGIE *crosses to the* GIRL *and* ALL OTHERS *move into a line looking over each other's shoulder.*) Hi!

GIRL. Hello.

GEORGIE. What's your name?

GIRL. Jill. What's yours?

GEORGIE. George.

GIRL. George what?

GEORGIE. Just George. You wanna play?

GIRL. Play? Can I? Can I finally play?

GEORGIE. Sure. (*He kisses her on the cheek or forehead.*)

GIRL. Oh, thank you.

GEORGIE. It's nothing. (*He crosses back toward the* GIRLS.) See there? I did it!

ALL. Good old, funny old Georgie.

GEORGIE. I'd even kiss a pig on a dare.

GIRL. Oh! How could you do that to me? (*She starts to cry.*)

TOOTIE. Look, she's crying.

ALL.

> Georgie, Porgie, Puddin' and Pie,
> Kissed the Girl and made her cry . . .

GEORGIE. The whole bunch of you are telling a lie. So shut up or I'll punch you in the eye.

TOOTIE. Oh, myyyyy!

ALL.

> Roses are red, violets are blue;
> Georgie's a spoil sport, so phooey on you.

GEORGIE. (*Facing front.*) "Sticks and stones may break my bones, but names will never hurt me."

PHOEBE. If you're gonna be nasty we won't play.

WANDA *and* FORDA. So pack your things and go away.

FLIRT. I think I hear your mother calling you, Georgie.

TOOTIE. (*In high voice with hand to mouth.*) Georgieee . . .

GEORGIE. She isn't, either.
WANDA *and* FORDA. 'Bye, Georgie-Porgie.
GEORGIE. I wanna stay.
ALL. 'Bye, Georgie! (ALL *wave*.)
GEORGIE. Please!
ALL. (*Definitely*.) Goodbye! (*They stick out their tongues, make faces and a "raspberry" noise, and he runs off fearfully. They* ALL *look at each other, unhappily. There is a pause while they amble to their places*.)
TOOTIE. What'll we do now?
DIDI. Make mud pies?
FLIRT. Sand castles?
WANDA. We're too old for that!
PHOEBE. Ring some doorbells?
FORDA. Steal old lady Brown's apples?
WANDA. We're too old for that, too.
TOOTIE. Then, what'll we do?
FLIRT. What'll we do?
PHOEBE. What'll we do?
WANDA. (*Rising*.) I'll tell you what let's do.
ALL. What let's do?
WANDA. Let's have a snipe hunt.
ALL. (*Crossing to form a semi-circle above* WANDA.) A snipe hunt! A snipe hunt!
DIDI. It's the best season for snipe hunts.
PHOEBE. My brother says the season's ripe for snipe.
WANDA. Now I know just the person to put in charge of catching them. (*She points toward the* GIRL.)
ALL. (*Together*.) Yes, just the person . . . THE GIRL WITH THE FUNNY NOSE!

(TOOTIE *leads* EVERYONE *over to the* GIRL. *They form a line behind* TOOTIE.)

TOOTIE. Hi. We wanna say we're sorry. Don't we?
ALL. Yes. We're sorry.
TOOTIE. And we want you to play a game.
GIRL. You do?
DIDI. Yes, we want you to play a game with us.

WANDA. And you're gonna be in charge.
FORDA. Yeah, in charge.
GIRL. What do I do?
DIXIE. It's a snipe hunt.
GIRL. A snipe hunt?
ALL. Yeah, a snipe hunt!
FORDA. And you're in charge.
GIRL. Oh, boy! But what do I do?
WANDA. You take this bag . . . and you open it wide like this. See?
GIRL. I see.
ALL. (*Together.*) Ho, ho, hee, hee, she see-s.
WANDA. And you stand in the middle of the playground with this bag.
GIRL. (*Running to Center of Stage.*) Oh, boy. Will anyone be helping?
WANDA. Oh, yes. We all go off and make a lot of noise scaring them out of the bushes. Then, when they run your way, you catch them.
GIRL. But what if they don't run my way?
PHOEBE. Then, you'll just be standing there all by yourself holding the bag.
ALL. *Phoe-be!*
WANDA. Everybody ready?
GIRL. All ready.
ALL. *Allll* . . . ready!
TOOTIE. Ready . . . All!
WANDA. Then, let's all go snipe hunting. Fee fum foe fipe, I smell the blood of a great big snipe.

(*They* ALL *quickly line up behind each other, crouched over as in a snake dance.*)

ALL.
>   Fee fum foe fipe!
>   We smell the blood of a great big snipe!

(*They circle the* GIRL *and head Offstage, repeating this*

into the distance, growing faster, but softer as they exit. The GIRL stands in the middle of the Stage happily looking around expectantly. She moves a little this way and a little that, crossing Down Right, Up Left and Down Left, listening carefully. Then, in the distance we faintly hear: "Ha, ha, ha, ha, ha." Her smile fades, she looks a little sad, then her lip begins to quiver and she starts to sob and fold her paper bag. She slowly picks up her tin can from the bench, crosses and sits sadly on the platform. After a moment we hear someone kicking a can. The GIRL looks up and, after a moment, a BOY enters kicking a can and carrying a brown paper bag. He has a funny nose just like the GIRL's.)

BOY. Hi.

GIRL. Hi.

BOY. (*Holding up his paper bag.*) Snipe hunt? (*She nods and half smiles.*) Me, too.

GIRL. Get any?

BOY. Nope. You?

GIRL. Afraid not. (*They both chuckle.*)

BOY. (*Touching nose.*) And they said I wasn't a regular guy, 'cause I was different. (*Slight pause while they both think. She nods.*) May I sit down? (*She nods, he sits by her.*) My name's Johnny.

GIRL. I knew it. I knew it all the time.

BOY. How?

GIRL. I don't know. I just did . . . somehow.

BOY. What's your name?

GIRL. Guess.

BOY. Juliet?

GIRL. No.

BOY. Victoria? Helen of Troy?

GIRL. No, silly. It's a very simple name.

BOY. Uhhh . . . Jill?

GIRL. Yes, yes. How'd you guess?

BOY. (*Proudly.*) Actually, I knew it as soon as I saw you.

GIRL. How?

BOY. Only a boy with a handsome nose like mine could recognize a girl with a pretty nose like yours, and be named Johnny and Jill.

GIRL. But it isn't pretty—it's ugly—and it's funny.

BOY. It isn't either ugly, and it isn't funny. Didn't anyone ever tell you how pretty you are?

GIRL. No. Why would anyone ever tell me that?

BOY. Because you are. You're Juliet and Cleopatra and you're—uh, you're—Lady Godiva!

GIRL. And you're crazy.

BOY. And you're cute.

GIRL. I have a funny nose.

BOY. I don't think it's funny.

GIRL. You're blind.

BOY. It's a beautiful nose.

GIRL. It's a funny nose.

BOY. Only because you think it's funny.

GIRL. Everybody says so.

(The LIGHTS begin to fade.)

BOY. Then, everybody's blind. It may be different, but it's not funny. Do you mind being different?

GIRL. Not any more. Do you?

BOY. Not any more.

GIRL. (*Rising.*) Ooooh, it's getting dark. I better go.

BOY. (*Rising.*) Can I walk you home?

GIRL. I'd feel honored. (*They start slowly to Right.*)

BOY. Jill, would you go somewhere with me?

GIRL. Where?

BOY. I don't know. To the moon. To New York.

GIRL. You can't take me to the moon, Johnny. And you can't even take me to New York.

BOY. Well, then, would you go with me to a movie?

GIRL. Maybe.

BOY. And would you sit in the balcony and hold my hand?

GIRL. (*Putting her hands behind her.*) No.

Boy. Why not?

Girl. 'Cause.

Boy. That's no reason. Please.

Girl. Why should I?

Boy. Just because it's that time of year. Will you?

Girl. No! Not unless we see a falling star.

Boy. All right. Let's look. (*They look up and out.*) The milky way's gonna be awful bright tonight.

Girl. Ummm . . .

Boy. Look!

Girl. What? Where?

Boy. (*Following its fall.*) There! There! A falling star!

Girl. Oh! It is!

Boy. Now will you go to a movie with me and hold my hand?

Girl. Well . . . all right. Yes! (*Slight pause.*)

Boy. And what kind of a nose do you have?

Girl. A nose just like yours. . . . (*She chuckles.*) Funny!

(*They* Both *laugh, and he takes her hand and they walk off slowly, leaving the Stage bare except for their two tin cans sitting side by side on the large platform s the LIGHTS fade to a blackout.*)

CURTAIN

GENERAL PRODUCTION NOTES

There is a very wide latitude of possibility—physically and vocally—for the imaginative director. Some stage directions are given, where it seemed that a suggestion or symbolic movement might be helpful. But not all movement is given nor does the director need to feel held to these.

It is good if there is an ever alive, ever changing and varied look to the stage. Use full backs, profiles, levels: top of the ladder, platforms and benches, sit and lie on the floor and platforms and benches. Use color and movement, realistic and stylized, as much as possible—as long as they are not distracting from the mood and feeling of the play.

It will help both the director and actor if he establishes a general "home base" area. For instance, the GIRL sits on the bench at left, DIXIE is around the big platform and WANDA is around the ladder. TOOTIE is a follower and friend of WANDA'S.

At the beginning of the play to insure all of the group starting together, pick a leader or someone who can be seen or heard to "start the group" with some "signal." This "signal" can be the nod of a head, clearing of the throat or snap of the fingers. It is only a matter of experimenting until something satisfactory is arrived at for your production. But don't leave it to chance or it will be ragged.

Sometimes there is a simple stage direction which reads "They all laugh." And at other times it will read "ALL. (They all laugh—separately) Ha, ha, ha, ha, ha!" And while both were intended to be treated realistically and the same, it is possible to treat the second way more stylistically in a particular production if it seems to be more appropriate.

While certain characters say certain things in their own way, that is, springing from their individual character—others are only spokesmen for the Group. And the general group comment by one character may be given to another character if the sound or balance of voices is improved by the change.

SETTINGS: The suggested setting is a symbolic, rather than actual, look at a playground. The back wall may have writing or posters on it. The floor may have hopscotch markings or drawn circles. The ladder is a "sort of" jungle gym. The platforms could be anything—perhaps a rock or embankment. The two benches may be, instead, two boxes or platforms on which to sit. The chinning rings can be two deck tennis rings hung from a batten by elastic so they can stretch down and then snap back out of the way.

PROPERTY LIST

Baseball equipment (optional):
    bat, glove(s), ball .... DIXIE, WANDA, FORDA, DIDI

Large bright handkerchief .... TOOTIE

Comic books .... DIDI, PHOEBE (DIXIE)

Playing cards .... DIXIE (PHOEBE)

Matchsticks .... DIXIE, PHOEBE

Chewing gum (optional) .... GEORGIE TO GIRLS

2 brown paper bags .... WANDA TO GIRL, THE BOY

2 tin cans, mashed and painted some bright
    color .... THE GIRL, THE BOY

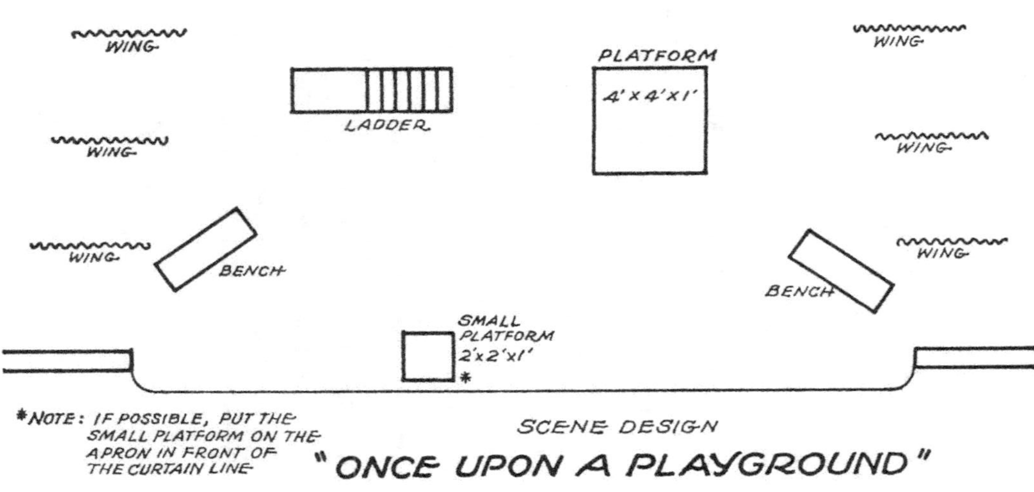

BACK WALL OR DRAPES
WING
WING
WING
LADDER
PLATFORM
4' x 4' x 1'
WING
WING
WING
BENCH
BENCH
SMALL
PLATFORM
2' x 2' x 1'
*
*NOTE: IF POSSIBLE, PUT THE
SMALL PLATFORM ON THE
APRON IN FRONT OF
THE CURTAIN LINE
SCENE DESIGN
" ONCE UPON A PLAYGROUND "

This work is published by Samuel French, an imprint of Concord Theatricals Corp.

No one shall make any changes in this title(s) for the purpose of production. No part of this book may be reproduced, stored in a retrieval system, scanned, uploaded, or transmitted in any form, by any means, now known or yet to be invented, including mechanical, electronic, digital, photocopying, recording, videotaping, or otherwise, without the prior written permission of the publisher. No one shall share this title(s), or any part of this title(s), through any social media or file hosting websites.

For all inquiries regarding motion picture, television, online/digital and other media rights, please contact Concord Theatricals Corp.

MUSIC AND THIRD-PARTY MATERIALS USE NOTE

Licensees are solely responsible for obtaining formal written permission from copyright owners to use copyrighted music and/or other copyrighted third-party materials (e.g. artworks, logos) in the performance of this play and are strongly cautioned to do so. If no such permission is obtained by the licensee, then the licensee must use only original music and materials that the licensee owns and controls. Licensees are solely responsible and liable for clearances of all third-party copyrighted materials, including without limitation music, and shall indemnify the copyright owners of the play(s) and their licensing agent, Concord Theatricals Corp., against any costs, expenses, losses and liabilities arising from the use of such copyrighted third-party materials by licensees. For music, please contact the appropriate music licensing authority in your territory for the rights to any incidental music.

IMPORTANT BILLING AND CREDIT REQUIREMENTS

If you have obtained performance rights to this title, please refer to your licensing agreement for important billing and credit requirements.